DENDE MARO:
The Golden Prince

Text and Illustrations
Copyright © Sally Mallam, 2009

First Edition 2009

Published by Hoopoe Books,
a division of The Institute for the Study of Human Knowledge

Visit www.hoopoekids.com
for a complete list of Hoopoe titles, CDs, DVDs,
an introduction on the use of Teaching-Stories
by Idries Shah and parent/teacher guides.

ISBN: 978-1-933779-48-5

A full CIP record for this book is available from the Library of Congress.

DENDE MARO:
The Golden Prince

by Sally Mallam
Illustrations created from the ancient rock art of Africa

To the children of Africa,
young and old.

More than a thousand million
years ago,
at a time before time,
when space was no space,
and when everything was nothing,
all that existed
was a longing.

This longing
grew
and grew.
It grew so strong
that it became a wind.

With every breath
the wind was hopeful,
and with every sigh
the wind said:

"I long to create a shape
that could become
the beginning
of all shapes."

... And it did.

The wind carried the shape
for miles and miles.

And a long time passed...

Then the sighing of the wind
awoke the shape, and in its
breath she heard the
longing,

and understood.

So the shape stirred.
She twirled and turned,
stretched and pulled,
and eventually...

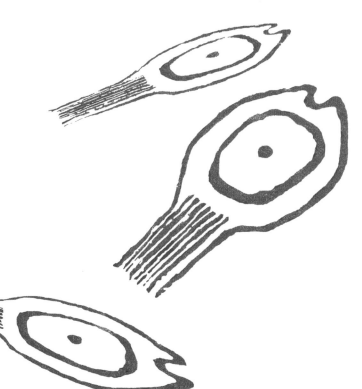

she became the shape
of the sky and
of everything in the sky.

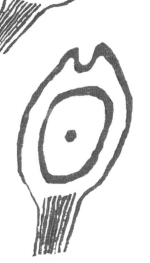

She became the shape of the sea

and of all that is in the sea.

She became the shapes
of the mountains,
the hills and valleys
of the land,
and of everything that grows
on the land.

She became the shapes
of all the animals
in the world,
from the enormous
elephant
to the tiny
ant.

And finally, she
became the shapes
of all the people
in the world.

It took a long, long
time for the shape
to do all this...

but she did.

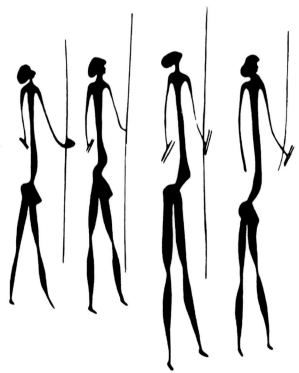

When the people of the world
looked around, they saw
the sky,
the sea,
and the land,
and they said:

"This is wonderful, but we long
for a guide who will tell us
how to live on the sea
and in the sea,
on the land,
and with the plants and animals."

Their longing grew and grew.
It grew so strong that a golden
prince was born.

His name was Dende Maro.

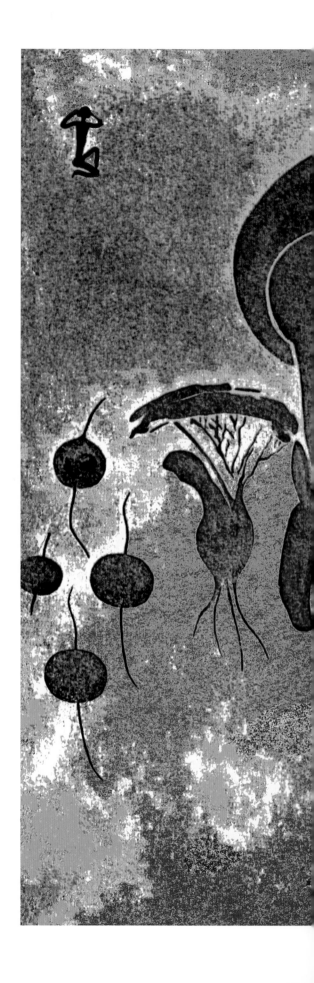

Prince Dende Maro taught the people
how to fish
in the sea,
the rivers,
and the streams
and how to swim in deep waters.

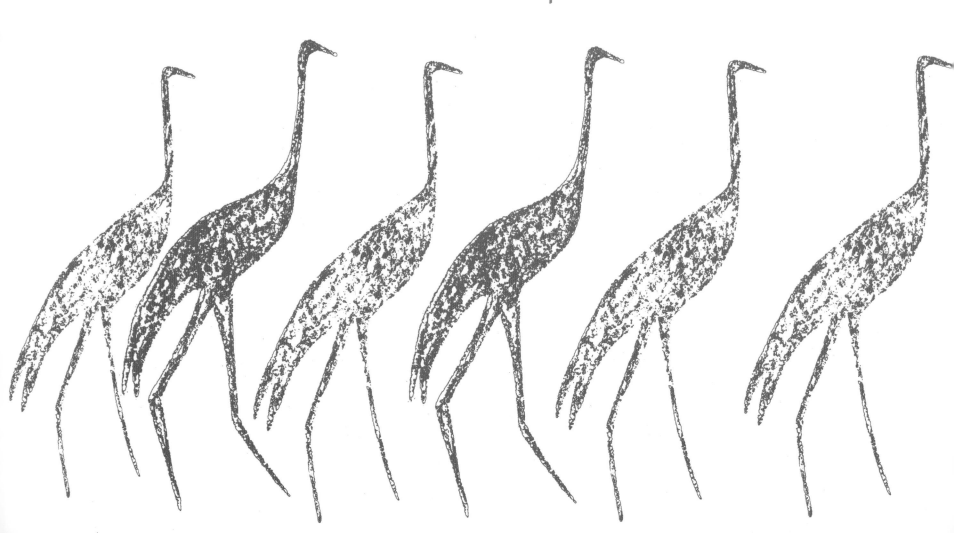

He showed them how to recognize
which plants were food and which were not,

how to cultivate land, plant seeds, and harvest crops.
Then he taught them how to care for all the animals and for each other.

Finally, the golden prince taught the people
how to travel by the stars in the sky.

And they journeyed
to the North,
the South,
the East,
and the West.

And they were never lost.

Thousands of years passed...

and once more the people felt a longing,
and this longing grew and grew.
It grew so strong that Dende Maro heard it
and he knew that the time was right
to call the people to him...

so he did.

And they came from the North,
the South,
the East,
and the West.

Then he showed them how to grind the colors of the earth
into fine powders and how to mix these colors with oils
from plants and animals.

He taught them how to dip their hands,
their hair,
and sticks in these colors
and to paint what they saw.

He showed them how to sharpen stones and shells,
and with them to carve images
of the sky,
the sea,
the land,
the animals,
and themselves.

Dende Maro
taught the people
how to listen in their
heart to the many
rhythms of the world.

And with shaped
wood and stretched
animal skin,
he showed them
how to drum
and to dance
to these rhythms.

So the people learned
how music would lift
their spirits and ease
their tiredness.

When, at last, the golden prince saw that the people
were ready, he taught them how to make other marks,
and each mark had a different meaning.

He called some marks numbers,
and he showed them how to count and to calculate.
He called other marks letters,
and he showed them how
letters make words,
how words make poems and stories
and record memories and dreams.

It took the people a very long time to learn all these things...

but they did.

They went back to
the North, the South
the East, and
the West
and searched for
places where they
could create their
images and marks,
away from the sun,
the wind, and the rain.

They found sheltered
rocks to carve and
to paint on and caves
with cool walls.

They took firelight
into the caves and
made their marks
and images there.

They carved and
colored the animals
and the plants.

They painted images of themselves by day
and of their shadows by night.

They painted their fortunes and misfortunes,
their fears, and their dreams.

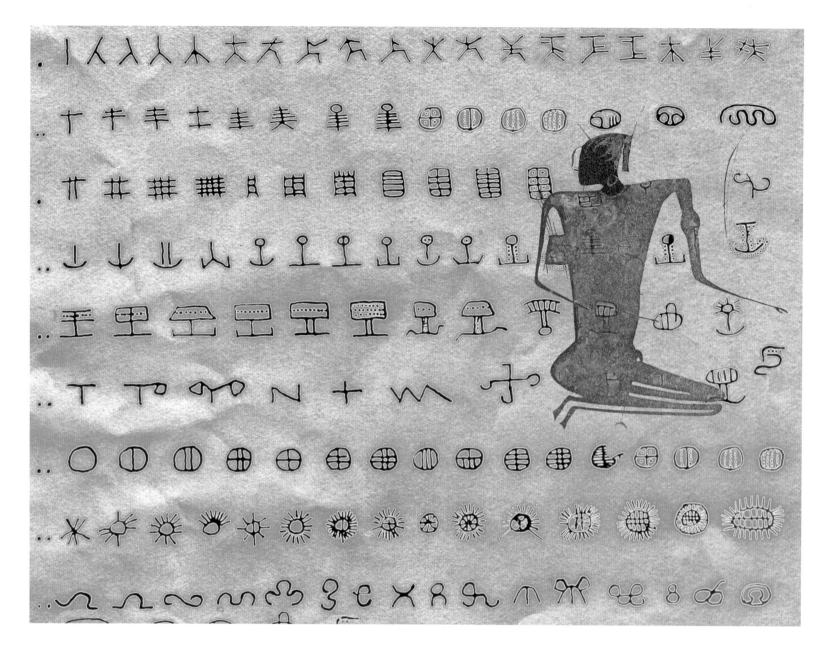

They wrote of their heroic deeds and sacrifices and of their travels.
They told of all they had seen and what they had learned.

They told of a golden prince,
whose name was Dende Maro,
who comes to people
when their longing is strong …

who taught them long, long ago
how to care for the animals
and for each other,
and who showed them
how to live well
in this wonderful world.

The End

The oldest dated human-made image as yet discovered is a small piece of incised ochre from the Blombos Cave in South Africa that is between 75,000 to 100,000 years old.

Rock art on the African continent has been found at thousands of sites, from South Africa, Namibia, and Zimbabwe in the south, to Zambia near the center, Tanzania in the east, Nigeria and Niger in the west, and on sheltered rock faces in the Sahara Desert, which was a fertile plain until around 2,500 B.C. The paintings and engravings in the Sahara are up to 10,000 years old. Some depict the arrival of cattle in North Africa between 4,500 and 4,000 B.C.

Dende Maro is the name given to the stone blocks or "thrones" at Rusape in Mashonaland, Zimbabwe, where the original figure, painted on rock, was found.

—Sally Mallam

Some of the countries
on the African continent
where ancient rock art
has been found.

For more information about African Rock Art, see these websites:

General Overview:

http://www.africanrockart.org/home/

http://www.bradshawfoundation.com/africa/

http://www.metmuseum.org/toah/hd/sroc/hd_sroc.htm

Sahara:

http://www.paleologos.com/mysterio.htm

Sub-Sahara (Nigeria Mali Niger Burkina Faso):

http://rupestre.net/tracce/subsaha.html

South Africa:

http://www.ruf.rice.edu/Rraar/ImagesSAI.html

Bibliography

Breuil, Henri, FOUR HUNDRED CENTURIES OF CAVE ART. Translated by Mary E. Boyle. Centre d'etudes et de documentation prehistoriques, Montignac (France), 1952.

Brentjdes, Burchard, AFRICAN ROCK ART. Translated by Anthony Dent. Fifty-six drawings by Hans-Ulric Herold, J.M. Dent & Sons Ltd., 1969.

Bandi, Hans-Georg & others, THE ART OF THE STONE AGE; FORTY THOUSAND YEARS OF ROCK ART. Translated by Ann E. Keep, Crown Publishers, Inc., N.Y., 1961.

Cooke, Cranmer Kenrick, ROCK ART OF SOUTHERN AFRICA, NATIONAL MUSEUM AND MONUMENTS OF RHODESIA. Longman Rhodesia (Pyt) Ltd., 1969.

Davidson, Basil, AFRICAN KINGDOMS, Time-Life Books, 1971.

Fairservis, Walter Ashlin, CAVE PAINTINGS OF THE GREAT HUNTERS, (New York) Museum Reproductions, 1955.

Frobenius, Leo, DIE AFRICKANISCHEN FELSBILDER. Vols 1, 11 and 111, Akademische Druck u. Verlagsanstalt, Graz, Austria, 1962

Goodall, Elizabeth, PREHISTORIC ROCK ART OF THE FEDERATION OF RHODESIA & NYASALAND. Paintings and descriptions by Elizabeth Goodall, C.K. Cooke, and J. Desmond Clark, edited by Roger Summers, National Publications Trust, Rhodesia and Nyasaland, 1959.

Johnson, Townley, R., Hyme Rabinowitz, & Percy Sieff, ROCK PAINTINGS OF THE SOUTH-WEST CAPE. Nasionale Boekhandel BPK, Cape Town, 1959.

Johnson, Townley, R., ROCK PAINTINGS OF SOUTHERN AFRICA, David Philip, Publisher (PTY) Ltd., 1979.

Lajoux, Jean-Dominique, TASSILI N'AJJER: ART RUPESTRE E CULTURE DE LA SAHARA PREHISTORIQUE, Editions du Chene, Paris, 1977.

Leakey, Mary, AFRICA'S VANISHING ART, THE ROCK PAINTINGS OF TANZANIA, Doubleday & Co., Inc., 1983.

Lewis -Williams, David, J., THE ROCK ART OF SOUTH AFRICA, Cambridge University Press, 1983.

Lhote, Henri, THE SEARCH FOR THE TASSILI FRESCOES, THE ROCK PAINTINGS OF THE SAHARA, E.P. Dutton & Co., 1959.

Mauny, Raymond, GRAVURES, PEINTURES ET INSCRIPTIONS RUPESTRES DE L'OUEST AFRICAIN, Institu Francais d'Afrique Noire, Dakar, 1937.

Mazonowicz, Douglas, VOICES FROM THE STONE AGE, A SEARCH FOR CAVE AND CANYON ART, Thomas Y. Crowell Co., New York, 1974.

Mori, Fabrizio, TADRART ACACUS; ARTE RUPESTRE E CULTURE DEL SAHARA PREISTORICO, Prefazione di Paolo Graziosi, Einaudi, Torino, 1965.

Nelson, Nels Christian, SOUTH AFRICAN ROCK PAINTINGS, Guide Leaflet Series of the American Museum of Natural History, #93, 1937.

Samachson, Dorothy and Joseph, THE FIRST ARTISTS, Doubleday & Co., New York, 1970.

Scherz, Ernst Rudolf & Annaliese, AFRICANISCHE FELSKUNST: MALEREIEN AUF FELSEN IN SUDWEST AFRICA, Verlag M. DuMont Schauberg, 1974.

Smith, Benjamin, W. ZAMBIA'S ANCIENT ROCK ART, PAINTINGS OF KASAMA, National Heritage Conservation Commission, Nuffield Press, Zambia, 1997.

Slack, Lina M., ROCK ENGRAVINGS FROM DRIEKOPS EILAND AND OTHER SITES SOUTH-WEST OF JOHANNESBURG, Compiled by Penelope A. Bennett with an introductory paper by C. Van Riet Lowe, Centaur Press Ltd., 1962.

Willcox, A.R., THE ROCK ART OF SOUTH AFRICAN, Thomas Nelson & Sons (Africa) Pty. Ltd., 1963.